# But, Mum!

First published in 2006 by
Franklin Watts
338 Euston Road
London
NW1 3BH

Franklin Watts Australia
Hachette Children's Books
Level 17/207 Kent Street
Sydney
NSW 2000



A CIP catalogue record for this book is available from the British Library.

ISBN (10) 0 7496 6595 5 (hbk)
ISBN (13) 978-0-7496-6595-1 (hbk)
ISBN (10) 0 7496 6812 1 (pbk)
ISBN (13) 978-0-7496-6812-9 (pbk)

**Series Editor:** Jackie Hamley
**Series Advisor:** Dr Barrie Wade
**Series Designer:** Peter Scoulding

Printed in China

# But, Mum!

by Ann Bryant

Illustrated by Kate Sheppard

"There's a spider
in the bath, Mum,

and its legs are
long and hairy!"

"Well, move it then!" said Mum.

“Yes, but Mum,
it’s really scary!”

"Well, catch it in a mug!" said Mum.

“But which mug shall I get?”

"Any mug will do. It's just a spider, don't forget!"

"The mugs are really high up, Mum!"

"Then go and fetch a chair!"

"But Mum, the chair is heavy and it won't move anywhere!"

"Well, ask your dad to help!" said Mum.

“But Dad will
just say: ‘Try!’

"And he's so busy sweeping leaves."

“Yes,” said Mum,
“and so am I!”

"Ask if you can help to sweep, while Dad helps move the chair."

"Dad! I'll help you sweep the ... whoops!"

“Jamie, why are you down there?”

"Mum, I'm really dirty.
Look!"

“Oh Jamie!
Did you fall?”

"Well go and have a wash," said Mum.

"But Mum, the sink is
far too small."

“Oh dear,” said Mum.
“Well, have a bath and
then come down for tea.”

"But Mum, there's something you've forgotten ..."

"There's this great big spider. See!"

**Leapfrog has been specially designed to fit the requirements of the National Literacy Strategy. It offers real books for beginning readers by top authors and illustrators.**

There are 55 Leapfrog stories to choose from:

**The Bossy Cockerel**
ISBN 0 7496 3828 1

**Bill's Baggy Trousers**
ISBN 0 7496 3829 X

**Mr Spotty's Potty**
ISBN 0 7496 3831 1

**Little Joe's Big Race**
ISBN 0 7496 3832 X

**The Little Star**
ISBN 0 7496 3833 8

**The Cheeky Monkey**
ISBN 0 7496 3830 3

**Selfish Sophie**
ISBN 0 7496 4385 4

**Recycled!**
ISBN 0 7496 4388 9

**Felix on the Move**
ISBN 0 7496 4387 0

**Pippa and Poppa**
ISBN 0 7496 4386 2

**Jack's Party**
ISBN 0 7496 4389 7

**The Best Snowman**
ISBN 0 7496 4390 0

**Eight Enormous Elephants**
ISBN 0 7496 4634 9

**Mary and the Fairy**
ISBN 0 7496 4633 0

**The Crying Princess**
ISBN 0 7496 4632 2

**Jasper and Jess**
ISBN 0 7496 4081 2

**The Lazy Scarecrow**
ISBN 0 7496 4082 0

**The Naughty Puppy**
ISBN 0 7496 4383 8

**Freddie's Fears**
ISBN 0 7496 4382 X

## FAIRY TALES

**Cinderella**
ISBN 0 7496 4228 9

**The Three Little Pigs**
ISBN 0 7496 4227 0

**Jack and the Beanstalk**
ISBN 0 7496 4229 7

**The Three Billy Goats Gruff**
ISBN 0 7496 4226 2

**Goldilocks and the Three Bears**
ISBN 0 7496 4225 4

**Little Red Riding Hood**
ISBN 0 7496 4224 6

**Rapunzel**
ISBN 0 7496 6159 3

**Snow White**
ISBN 0 7496 6161 5

**The Emperor's New Clothes**
ISBN 0 7496 6163 1

**The Pied Piper of Hamelin**
ISBN 0 7496 6164 X

**Hansel and Gretel**
ISBN 0 7496 6162 3

**The Sleeping Beauty**
ISBN 0 7496 6160 7

**Rumpelstiltskin**
ISBN 0 7496 6165 8

**The Ugly Duckling**
ISBN 0 7496 6166 6

**Puss in Boots**
ISBN 0 7496 6167 4

**The Frog Prince**
ISBN 0 7496 6168 2

**The Princess and the Pea**
ISBN 0 7496 6169 0

**Dick Whittington**
ISBN 0 7496 6170 4

**The Elves and the Shoemaker**
ISBN 0 7496 6575 0*
ISBN 0 7496 6581 5

**The Little Match Girl**
ISBN 0 7496 6576 9*
ISBN 0 7496 6582 3

**The Little Mermaid**
ISBN 0 7496 6577 7*
ISBN 0 7496 6583 1

**The Little Red Hen**
ISBN 0 7496 6578 5*
ISBN 0 7496 6585 8

**The Nightingale**
ISBN 0 7496 6579 3*
ISBN 0 7496 6586 6

**Thumbelina**
ISBN 0 7496 6580 7*
ISBN 0 7496 6587 4

## RHYME TIME

**Squeaky Clean**
ISBN 0 7496 6805 9

**Craig's Crocodile**
ISBN 0 7496 6806 7

**Felicity Floss: Tooth Fairy**
ISBN 0 7496 6807 5

**Captain Cool**
ISBN 0 7496 6808 3

**Monster Cake**
ISBN 0 7496 6809 1

**The Super Trolley Ride**
ISBN 0 7496 6810 5

**The Royal Jumble Sale**
ISBN 0 7496 6594 7*
ISBN 0 7496 6811 3

**But, Mum!**
ISBN 0 7496 6595 5*
ISBN 0 7496 6812 1

**Dan's Gran's Goat**
ISBN 0 7496 6596 3*
ISBN 0 7496 6814 8

**Lighthouse Mouse**
ISBN 0 7496 6597 1*
ISBN 0 7496 6815 6

**Big Bad Bart**
ISBN 0 7496 6599 8*
ISBN 0 7496 6816 4

**Ron's Race**
ISBN 0 7496 6600 5*
ISBN 0 7496 6817 2

* hardback